W9-CLF-489

ALIEN IN MY POCKET

Radio Active

by
Nate Ball

illustrated by
Macky Pamintuan

HARPER
An Imprint of HarperCollinsPublishers

Library of Congress Cataloging-in-Publication Data
Ball, Nate.
    Radio active / by Nate Ball ; [illustrated by Macky Pamintuan]. — First edition.
        pages cm. — (Alien in my pocket)
    Summary: Plans go awry when Amp, the four-inch-tall lead scout from the planet Erde, uses parts from fourth-grader Zack's walkie-talkie to build a quantum radio to alert his commanders to call off the pending invasion of Earth. Includes directions for building a radio.
    ISBN 978-0-06-231493-2 (trade bdg.) — ISBN 978-0-06-221627-4 (pbk.)
    [1. Extraterrestrial beings—Fiction. 2. Friendship—Fiction. 3. Radio broadcasting—Fiction. 4. Schools—Fiction.] I. Pamintuan, Macky, illustrator. II. Title.
PZ7.B1989Rad 2014   2013037270
[Fic]—dc23   CIP
                                                                                                      AC

Typography by Sean Boggs
14 15 16 17 18 LP/RRDH 10 9 8 7 6 5 4 3 2 1
❖
First Edition

Contents

01

Shipwrecked

I bet when you imagine somebody who has been shipwrecked, you think of a really skinny guy with a scraggly beard, eating bananas on a tiny island.

I know I would have before Amp arrived.

Amp is the alien who got shipwrecked in my room.

I kid you not.

Amp crash-landed on planet Earth through my bedroom window. His spaceship smashed my bedroom wall and landed on my bed. I had to cover the blackened dent in my wall with a baseball poster so my mom didn't see it. I still haven't really explained the black stains on my sheets.

But those are the least of my problems. Now I have a blue alien not much bigger than my fist

1

secretly living in my room. Imagine trying to keep that a secret! Not easy, especially since instead of bananas, my stranded traveler only eats Ritz crackers and SweeTarts. Seriously, there's only so many rolls of SweeTarts a kid can buy without people starting to get suspicious!

You might think living with your own little alien dude is fascinating and incredible and amazing—but you'd be wrong. It's like sharing your room with an annoying little brother. A little, blue, three-fingered brother from another planet. I already have a little brother from this planet. And trust me, one little brother is more than enough.

"Did you fart?" my alien houseguest asked, interrupting my homework—again.

"Whoever smelt it dealt it," I mumbled, not looking up from my math homework.

"How dare you?" Amp replied in his high-pitched voice. "You know my body uses energy much too efficiently to require the release of leftover gases."

"Oh, come on," I groaned.

"I am offended, Zack. I'm simply noting that

3

suddenly your room smells funny."

"You're always floating air biscuits and then pointing fingers."

"What do you mean by 'air biscuits'?"

"Oh, you know. A barking spider. A cheese squeeze. A thunder muffin. A seat tweet."

"I can honestly say I have no idea what you are talking about."

I put down my pencil and turned to look at him. "I am saying you release cloud monkeys all the time then act all mystified as to why it smells like burning tires in here. Face it, you fluff quite frequently because of that crummy diet of yours."

"I am still puzzled as to why my affection for Ritz crackers and SweeTarts troubles you so much."

"It wouldn't be so much of a problem if you didn't walk around like a crop duster, leaving a trail of toxic alien farts behind you."

Amp was quiet for a second. He sat down on the alarm clock next to my bed and squirmed. I think he was trying to give me some alien stink-eye, but it just made him look even more gassy.

"You can't prove a thing."

I rolled my eyes and turned back to my word problems. "Silent but deadly." I sighed.

"I heard that."

"Good," I whispered. "You little fart factory."

"I heard that, too."

The walkie-talkie next to my math book suddenly crackled to life. "Earth One, this is Earth Two. Over."

Olivia.

Olivia is my best friend and next-door neighbor, and she's the only other person on the planet who knows about my secret roommate.

I picked up the walkie-talkie and pushed the Talk button. "This is Earth One. Read you loud and clear. What's up? Over."

I stared at the walkie-talkie, waiting.

"I'm coming over. Over."

"Over? Oh, roger. Over," I said awkwardly.

"What?" Olivia responded after a few seconds. "I've got SweeTarts. Over."

"Oh, goodie, dinner," Amp said from behind me.

"You mean SweetFarts? Over."

"Funny. Over."

5

Then I heard the doorbell ring downstairs.

It was time for our daily meeting about getting Amp back home. We hadn't met in three days, though, so our daily meeting might need a new name.

02

Listen to This

"It smells like the devil burped in here."

Olivia had just shut the door of my room. She pulled two rolls of SweeTarts out of her pocket and tossed them to Amp, who was still sitting on my alarm clock.

"It smells like that because he keeps eating those fart pills," I said, still hunched over my math homework. "Hey, did you get the one about the train leaving San Francisco at eight p.m.?" I asked, turning around in my chair.

Olivia is in my class at Reed School. Schoolwork isn't difficult for her. Olivia just sort of knows stuff. She usually finishes her math homework while everyone else is packing up to leave for the day. She'd be a real brain if she weren't so weird and didn't talk so much.

"Forty-eight miles an hour is the answer," she said, watching Amp flip SweeTarts into his mouth.

"Forty-eight?" I croaked. "I have five hundred forty-four!"

"How is that possible?" She laughed, shaking her head at me. "What train travels that fast, Whacky Zacky?"

"Maybe those Japanese bullet trains. I saw them on TV."

"They don't go that fast," she corrected me. "Two hundred miles an hour, tops."

"We have trainlike vehicles back on Erde," Amp said, once again bragging about how great things were on his planet. "They travel about as fast as sound travels here."

"I've told you before about talking with your mouth full," I grumbled, turning back to my incorrect math problem. "You may have fast trains on Erde, but we have something called manners here on this planet."

"Has he been this grumpy the whole time?" Olivia asked Amp.

"Since he got home. Surprisingly, math makes him angry."

Honestly, all our meetings about fixing Amp's busted spaceship, getting him off this planet, and returning my life to normal went like this. What was the point of meeting if we never accomplished anything except pointing out all the things I do wrong? I was so not the problem.

There was a knock on my bedroom door. Olivia quickly moved to block the view of Amp from the doorway.

She always did this, even though Amp could easily make himself invisible to someone. He uses one of his Jedi mind tricks. He basically erases your memory of seeing him as you see him, so you instantly forget you're seeing him while you're looking at him.

I know, it sounds complicated. You get used to it. But Olivia always forgets he can do that.

The door clicked open and my little brother poked his head in.

"I heard you have SweeTarts," he said. "I want some."

"Go away, Taylor," I groaned from my desk. "We're busy."

Olivia reached into her pocket and tossed

Taylor a roll of SweeTarts. He intentionally missed the catch so he could step all the way into my room. "Hey, what are you guys doing?" he asked, looking around. "It smells like burning toothpaste in here."

Taylor knew something was up. He knew I was hiding a secret, and he'd dedicated his life to figuring out what it was. He'd even built an army of spy robots to help him. Fortunately, I'd destroyed most of them when I caught them in my room.

My parents are convinced Taylor is some kind of genius. He *is* only in the first grade and building robots. But I don't care. I think he's only a genius at annoying me.

I got up and pushed him out of my room. "Go play with your robots, you Nosy Nelly." I closed the door on him and leaned my back against it.

"But I want to hang out with you guys," he said from the other side of the door.

"Buzz off!" I shouted. I heard him walk down the squeaky hallway.

Olivia sat up on my bed. She had an odd look on her face. It was almost white, like she'd seen a ghost.

"What's wrong with you?" I ask. "Is Amp's gas cloud getting to you?"

"How did he know I had SweeTarts? I didn't tell him, and you didn't tell him, so how did he know?"

The three of us stared at each other.

Without looking down, Olivia unclipped the walkie-talkie from her pocket. She held it up and stared at it. "That little sneak is listening in on our walkie-talkie conversations."

"What a clever idea," Amp whispered.

I looked at them both. I was pretty sure steam was coming out of my ears. "A clever idea that the little worm is gonna pay for."

03

Let's Talk

As Amp studied the walkie-talkie on my desk, Olivia and I discussed ways to get back at Taylor.

Olivia lives with her grandfather in the house next to ours. He has a line he always says: "Turnabout is fair play." I always just thought he was weird, but for the first time, I understood what he meant. If Taylor was going to listen in on our conversations, we were going to make sure he heard what we wanted him to hear.

"We could have walkie-talkie conversations that convince Taylor that an evil spirit named Amp has taken over your body," Olivia suggested. "You could pretend to have a split personality."

"Or that I have an evil, secret twin brother who lives under my bed," I said. "So at breakfast he won't know if he's sitting across from me or my evil twin."

"What would your twin's name be?" Olivia asked. "Amp simply won't do."

"How about Herm?" I suggested.

"Herm is so good," she agreed. "Perfect."

We were both watching Amp check out my walkie-talkie. He often studied human technology with great interest; it seemed to amuse him half the time and puzzle him the other half.

He stroked his chin and walked around the thing like it was the most fascinating thing ever made on this planet.

"Maybe my twin's name could be Cooper," I said.

"That's a terrible name. Everyone would call him Pooper," she told me.

"Ah, man, I always liked that name."

"Wait, wait. Maybe we could say Amp is your secret pet tarantula!" Olivia said, clapping with excitement. "Taylor hates spiders."

"They make him turn as white as cream cheese," I agreed.

"Maybe it's one of those goliath bird-eater tarantulas from South America."

"That I ordered off the internet with six months of my allowance money!"

"Yeah! Oh, he'll look it up on the internet and freak out completely. That tarantula is seriously the size of your catcher's mitt."

"That'll serve him right," I said, nodding slowly as the plan took shape in my head. "And my tarantula will go missing. I won't be able to find him."

Olivia laughed. "You could say on the walkie-talkie that you think it may have escaped into

Taylor's room, but you're afraid to tell him or your parents. Wait till he hears that. Don't you wish you could see his face?"

We high-fived. It was a great plan.

But, as always happened in our meetings, we had not moved the ball forward one inch in terms of helping Amp repair his space-and-time-skipping ship.

I noticed Amp suddenly turn his back to us and speak in a quiet voice into the contraption he wore on his wrist.

"Note to Erdian Council: Humans utilize simple two-way radio transceivers they call walkie-talkies. They appear to utilize a range of between four and five hundred megahertz on what they call the ultrahigh frequency spectrum, or UHF for short."

"Amp, you're being rude," I said. "We can totally hear you." Taking verbal notes for his alien bosses on that thing was just one of his many annoying habits.

Amp continued:

"Primitive but effective construction. Limited range and poor battery life. But efficient. One of the earthlings' better devices–"

"I'm going to give you to my brother if you don't stop that creepy mumbling," I growled at him.

Amp turned back to face us, paused, and cleared his throat. "I have an idea that I'd like to share," he announced.

"No, we like the missing giant tarantula idea," Olivia said.

"It's pretty solid," I agreed. "You're not gonna top that one, blue man."

"This isn't about your childish plan for tricking Taylor," he said, shaking his head at us.

"Oh," Olivia and I said at the same time.

"Jinx," she said, and punched me in the arm a lot harder than you would think a girl could punch your arm.

"*Ow!*" I said, moving away from Olivia. I rubbed my arm. "What idea are you talking about then, Amp?"

"I am talking about forgetting about fixing my ship."

"*What?*" Olivia and I both said in unison.

Before I could move farther away, she punched me again in the same spot she had just seconds ago. "Jinx again!" she screamed.

"Stop it, Olivia!" I shouted, jumping up. "Never mess with a catcher's throwing arm. This is my ticket to the big leagues."

"Sorry," Olivia said with a giggle. She turned to the alien invader. "Ampy, what do you mean about not fixing your ship? Are you giving up?"

"You're not quitting!" I yelped. "If you don't call off the attack, your people are going to show up here and my life will never return to normal. You can't throw in the towel now!"

"I don't even have a towel," he said, looking around. He considered both of us like we had lost our minds. "I am talking about building a special kind of radio. A quantum radio—think of it as a supersized walkie-talkie—so that I can radio Erde from here and call off the invasion."

We were all quiet for a moment.

"Why didn't you think of this before?" I asked.

"My radio was damaged in the crash, but I may be able to use your walkie-talkie to work around it."

"Hey, we can still do the tarantula thing, right?" Olivia asked.

Amp sighed and shrugged his tiny shoulders. "I don't see why not."

Olivia held up her hand for another high five, but I wasn't able to move my arm yet.

04

Pet Trap

Olivia ate dinner at my house that night. She was doing that more and more often lately. Partly because her grandpa returned late when he went fishing, but really because my mom loved having Olivia over.

Olivia was the daughter she never had.

"Do you need more milk, sweetie?" Mom cooed in a soft, caring voice she never used on me.

"Oh, no thanks, Mrs. McGee, I've barely started drinking the one you already poured," Olivia answered.

"Call me Christine, dear," Mom gushed.

"Oh, okay . . . Christine," Olivia replied, obviously feeling uncomfortable.

"I could use some more milk, Christine," I said hopefully.

"It's in the fridge, dear," Mom answered, not looking up from the roll she was buttering.

We never had rolls with dinner unless Olivia was eating over.

"What do you guys do in there all day?" Taylor asked. He looked up from the steak he was trying to cut with an electric knife he had recently built.

It also seemed like we never had steak for dinner unless Olivia was eating over.

"We do homework," I said, shuffling to the fridge for more milk.

"Are you guys boyfriend and girlfriend?" Taylor asked.

"Taylor!" Mom cried.

"Enough of that," Dad said, looking sharply at Taylor, a piece of juicy steak hanging from his fork.

Olivia broke the awkward silence with a big laugh. I knew it was not her real laugh, but it fooled all of them. "Of course not, silly," she said. "We talk about homework, baseball, and the Young Volunteers."

"I want to be in the Young Volunteers, too," Taylor said.

"No, you don't," Olivia said. "Trust me."

"You have to be in the third grade at least," I said. "And I'm only doing it because Principal Luntz is making me. Which is probably illegal when you think about it."

"Yeah," Olivia agreed, pointing at me with her fork. "You're right, Zackaroni. I bet that club breaks forty different child labor laws."

"It's not illegal," Dad said, swirling his mashed potatoes with his fork.

"Why did the principal make you join the Young Volunteers again?" Taylor asked, looking around suspiciously.

"It involved a large slingshot and water balloons filled with spoiled milk," Olivia bragged, popping a piece of roll in her mouth.

"That unfortunate incident caused me a lot of trouble," Dad said, raising his eyebrows at Olivia.

"We had no idea Principal Luntz would be in the parking lot," I cut in.

"We actually knocked his glasses off," Olivia said happily.

"And broke them," Mom added quietly.

"Wow," Taylor said. "Why hasn't anybody told me this story before?"

"It's not the kind of thing we like to brag about," Dad said.

"He was more mad that the milk smelled terrible than that his glasses were broken," Olivia added.

I so wished we could stop talking about this.

Luntz had wanted to suspend us, but instead,

after a long, long, long meeting with my parents and Olivia's grandfather, he decided to make us join his Young Volunteers club. My dad called it a plea bargain we couldn't refuse, whatever that meant.

So now every month or so, Olivia and I have to "help" at community events. Sometimes it eats up an entire Saturday, which is pure torture. And Luntz has a mandatory attendance policy, no excuses allowed. You could be puking up a lung and he'd still make you count change at the library bake sale. It was a lot like serving a long prison sentence on your weekends.

"Luckily, we have only three weeks left," I said, feeling like I could see the light at the end of a very long and very dark tunnel.

"You shouldn't think of it that way," Mom said. "It is a volunteer club, after all. You are helping out your community."

"I agree with you, Christine," Olivia said. "But the problem is, there's nothing voluntary about it. We have to go. We're like Luntz's private army of do-gooders."

"Well, it sounds like fun to me," Taylor harrumphed.

"Just get in big trouble and you're in," Olivia advised. She looked around the table. "I'm just kidding, guys."

I kept my eyes on the prize. Olivia and I had to work this Saturday at the big half marathon they held every year in our town. Then we were pretty much done. I could leave Principal Luntz and his lame Young Volunteers club in my rearview mirror. I could almost taste sweet freedom already.

Little did I know that development would run into a major snag.

05

Spaced-out Radio

After dinner, Olivia and I went to hang out in her garage. Her grandfather kept a cool old car in there, plus a dusty old couch, some other random furniture, and about thirty fishing poles hanging from the rafters. It was a nice place to get away from the prying eyes of my brother.

"This plan may not work," Amp admitted as he examined Olivia's grandfather's tools. He found a screwdriver that was twice as tall as he was. He dragged it over to the walkie-talkie. He wanted to take off the back cover, but the screwdriver was too big for him to handle. I had to pluck it away before he hurt himself. I opened the back of the walkie-talkie while he walked in circles around it.

"I don't see how a walkie-talkie that can only work to the end of the street can call all the way

back to Erde," Olivia said.

"Yeah, Amp, this seems like one of your dumber ideas," I said.

"I beg your pardon," Amp said, putting his hands on his hips and glaring at me. "I do not have 'dumb ideas,' young earthling."

"Oh, so now I'm 'young earthling'?" I said, looking at Olivia and rolling my eyes. "Get a load of Mr. Bossy Blue Pants over here."

"Yes, as I was saying, it may not work," Amp sighed. "But it is worth a try. I think I can connect this device to the damaged quantum radio on the *Dingle*."

"On the what?" I croaked.

"What's a dingle?" Olivia asked.

Amp stared at us, his mouth hanging open. "I never told you?"

"Told us what?" Olivia said. "About your dingle?"

He stood up as tall as he could and lifted his chin high in the air. "The *Dingle*, may I inform you, is my spaceship," he said.

Olivia and I both cracked up.

"That is the worst name ever for a spaceship," Olivia said.

"Was the *Fart Rocket* already taken?" I laughed.

"How about the *Nerdy Erde Express?*" Olivia said, cracking us up even more.

"Go ahead and laugh it up," Amp said, clearly offended. "I'm stranded on this primitive planet and may not be able to prevent it from being invaded, but please, have a good laugh at my expense."

"Don't be so dang sensitive," I said. "But seriously, a walkie-talkie? There's got to be a better way."

"Yeah, how about smoke signals?" Olivia said.

"Or one of those carrier pigeons with a note tied around its leg," I said.

"Why don't we tie a note to a rock and throw it real hard?"

"You two are ridiculous," Amp fumed. "Always thinking small. Never considering the brains, wisdom, and creativity of my civilization."

I groaned. "Get off your high horse, short man. Our civilization would never name a spaceship the *Dingle*."

"Or visit another planet in a junky ship that can't make the return trip."

Amp waved at us in irritation and stared at the exposed guts of the walkie-talkie.

Amp seemed to get lost in examining the tiny parts of the device for a second time. After a few minutes, he looked up at us. "Where did you two get these walkie-talkies?"

"They're actually not ours," Olivia said.

"We get them for the Young Volunteers," I said. "For when we're working at events."

"They give us the walkie-talkies so they can tell us where to go and where we're needed," Olivia said. "It's a lot like jail, but they give you a radio."

"You both have a curious view of community service for your fellow humans."

I ignored his observation. "We have to return them when our prison sentence is up."

"But they let you keep them between events?" Amp asked.

"Yep," Olivia and I said at the same time.

Learning from experience, I leaped out of the way before Olivia could give me another charley horse. "Jinx!" she cried, but her knuckles missed their target.

I stuck my tongue out and danced a little. "Strike one, slowpoke."

"Please, you two, you're acting like children!"

"Last time I checked," Olivia said, "we *were* children." Then she started dancing and sticking her tongue out at me.

"Stop doing that!" Amp said. "You are making it hard to concentrate. I need to borrow one of these," Amp continued, putting the cover back on the walkie-talkie. He left it to me to put the screws in. "If my calculations are correct, I can connect it to the quantum radio on my ship and bypass the parts that aren't working. When is your next community activity?"

"Three days," Olivia said. "We're working at a half marathon race downtown."

"I'm in charge of all the portable toilets," I admitted.

"How exciting," Amp said flatly. "I should know before then if it's working or not. I'll return your walkie-talkie at the event."

"Okay, just don't start quite yet," I said. "Olivia and I need to have a chat tonight about a spider."

"Okay," he said in a strange, faraway voice. "I'll

start first thing tomorrow morning, while you two are in school."

I should have known then that Amp had no intention of keeping his word. How do you know when a blue alien is lying to you? His lips are moving.

35

06

Attack of the Amp!

"**O**h my gosh, Olivia, something terrible has happened," I said in my best fake-frightened voice. "Over," I added, pushing the Talk button again. I waited.

I was in bed with the lights off. I assumed Olivia was, too.

"Really? I cannot imagine what could have happened. Over," she said in a very fake-sounding voice. Boy, she was a terrible actress.

It was late, and my mom had just barged in, snapped off my light, pushed me into bed, and given me a peck on the forehead. "Sleep," she commanded as she shut my door.

Sleep was the last thing on my mind.

"You will not believe me," I said. "This is just terrible." I almost started laughing, but I let go of the button and covered my mouth with my free hand. I knew that my little brother was down the hall in his room listening in on this conversation. He'd pay for his snooping.

"I am freaking out over whatever has happened," Olivia's voice crackled suddenly. "But you haven't told me yet what it is that has happened," she added.

Could she be a worse actress?

"You know Amp?" I said, and released the button.

"Oh, Amp?" her voice asked over the speaker. "You mean your spider? Your gigantic, goliath South American bird-eating tarantula that you keep in your room and that you bought off the internet with six months of your allowance money? That Amp?"

I rolled my eyes. Too much information! She was trying too hard.

"Yes, my giant tarantula named Amp."

"It is as big as your catcher's mitt."

I growled. "I know how big it is, Olivia, it is my pet that I love so much."

"Sorry," her voice answered. "I do not love your tarantula. It scares me. It is so big that I can hear it breathe."

"No, you can't," I said. "That's ridiculous. I'm not even sure spiders breathe."

"Of course they breathe," she said in a snotty, sassy voice.

"Whatever!" I said, squeezing the Talk button so hard I thought it might crack. "It doesn't matter if he can breathe or not, Olivia! The point is that I have a huge, enormous spider named Amp, one I spent all my allowance money to get, and I don't know where he is. Got it?"

I gave her almost fifteen seconds to reply. "Listen up, Cranky Pants. I've heard of waking up on the wrong side of the bed, but I never heard of going to sleep on the wrong side of the bed."

"Oh, just shut up. Earth Two, over!"

I dropped the walkie-talkie on my blanket and grabbed my head. We should have rehearsed. This sounded totally dumb. Olivia could not act her way out of a paper bag! And she was getting me all tangled up in spider trivia. Who cares if a spider breathes or not?

I snatched up the walkie-talkie again. "Amp could be anywhere," I said, trying to sound scared. "I don't know what to do."

"When was the last time you saw him?" Olivia asked.

I thought about that one. What was the right answer? "Yesterday," I said, finally deciding. "He may have left my room. He could be in Taylor's room for all I know."

"I may have seen him in there yesterday," Olivia said in a whisper.

"You did?" I croaked, forgetting we were making this up.

Her response came quickly. "Yes. Over."

I couldn't think of anything else to say.

Then Olivia spoke again. "I said 'over,' you know."

"I know. Over."

"Should we tell him?" she asked. She sounded like she was getting bored.

"Tell who?"

"Who do you think? Your brother!"

"Oh," I said, getting it now. "Oh, no. We cannot tell him. He will be upset. He does not like spiders. Plus, he'll tell my mom and dad, and I will get in big trouble." I dropped the walkie-talkie and nodded. I was good at this.

"But your spider named Amp may eat your brother," Olivia's voice crackled back through the tiny speaker. It sounded like she was holding back a laugh.

"There's nothing funny about this."

"Oh, I know," she said back.

41

"Good night, Olivia," I said. "See you tomorrow morning. We will look for my spider tomorrow after school when Taylor is not around. It is probably in his room."

"Okay! Over!" Olivia sounded bored again.

I put the walkie-talkie on my nightstand and got cozy.

"That was ridiculous," Amp's voice said from the dark.

"That, my alien friend, was not ridiculous. That was revenge."

Before long, I drifted off to sleep, not knowing what disastrous events I had just put into motion.

07

Spider Fallout

Aside from the fact that I found Taylor asleep on the living room couch, Thursday morning proceeded like a normal day.

I grabbed some breakfast and was just gathering up my homework from my desk, when I heard Erdian bad words coming from my closet. I opened the door to find Amp at work inside his ship. And it obviously wasn't going so great.

"I'm off to school, Amp," I said, smiling.

"Floofy bolt!" I heard him squeak in frustration. *"Flab dabbler!"*

"Hey, watch your language in there," I said, holding back a giggle. Erde may be an uppity, advanced civilization in a galaxy far, far away, but they still have way more bad words than we do.

"I cannot work under these conditions," he

growled. "If I only had brought that *dabsnapping* molder flincher with me."

"Oh, hey, I think I might have a molder flincher around here somewhere," I said, unable to hold back my laughter any longer.

"Don't be such a doozle, Zack," he snapped, poking his head out of a hatch near the ship's front that I hadn't even noticed was open.

He looked like a blue gopher.

"Just so you know, our prank worked like a charm," I told him. "Taylor was so freaked he slept on the couch."

"All because of a spider?" he asked.

"All because of a spider," I agreed.

"Fascinating," he said, turning his back to me. He whispered into the contraption he wore on his wrist:

"Note to Erdian Council: Humans are afraid of spiders. Spiders are web-spinning, eight-legged arthropods. An arthropod's body is in sections. A spider's body has two sections. Most spiders also have

four eyes. Some have more. Weird. They are also smaller than the smallest Erdian. Perhaps we can use this information in planning our invasion."

"You know that not all humans are afraid of spiders," I interrupted.

"Agggh, you were listening?" Amp screamed.

"You weren't exactly being quiet."

"Stop being a doozle, Zack, and get to school. I have work to do."

"I'd play hooky and help you, buddy, but I can only fit about three fingers in there."

He glared at me. "*Blagh*," he said, waving a little tool at me and returning to his secret tinkering.

Once on the school bus, I almost felt bad for Taylor. He was sitting up front in his usual spot, but he was staring out the window instead of showing off some new gizmo he was working on. His head seemed to bob with sleepiness.

Then I remembered his meddling and snooping and spying. "Serves him right," I mumbled.

Olivia was trying to get me to watch her do coin tricks.

"Where'd it go?" she asked for the third time. "See? It's gone. Can you believe it? That's magic."

I just rolled my eyes.

"Don't be a hater, Zack."

I couldn't wait for her magic phase to end.

Olivia was curious about practically everything. Last week it was French. The week before that she was obsessed with an animal I had never heard of called a pangolin. Before that it was hypnosis, kite building, juggling, and a few long weeks when all she could talk about was how they built

47

the pyramids. She never stuck with anything for very long. That made her kind of fascinating—but exhausting.

"Oh my gosh, there's a coin in your ear," she said, pretending to pull a quarter out of my ear. "How did your empty head become a piggy bank?"

I stared at her with dull eyes. "Bleh," I said.

After slogging through math, social studies, and reading, my teacher, Miss Martin, announced that it was time for a mandatory Young Volunteers meeting. It was a prerace run-through. We reviewed schedules and responsibilities for tomorrow's race. About ten kids who had been caught in some misdeed or another squeezed into Principal Luntz's tiny conference room. The room smelled like bologna, apple juice, and boredom.

I counted Max Myers yawning seven times in one minute.

After reviewing who was doing what at the race, Principal Luntz asked us if everyone had tested their walkie-talkies as he had suggested in our last meeting.

Olivia and I looked at each other and smiled. We nodded.

Principal Luntz passed out our official volunteer badges and dismissed us, but he asked me to stay behind. He waved Olivia away when she tried to stay at my side.

"Remember, you have the right to a lawyer, Zack," she said, not helping me feel any better. "You have the right to remain silent, too." With a nod and a firm slap on my back, she exited.

I turned back to Principal Luntz, who had me fixed in an odd stare.

Did he know about Amp tearing apart my walkie-talkie?

Did he know I had blacked out one of Ben Franklin's front teeth in my history book?

Had he heard about the thunderous Cheerio-smelling burp I launched the day before during reading time?

My heart tap-danced. My stomach shrank. My armpits got moist.

"Zack, can you tell me anything about this note?" he asked, handing me a note written on a torn piece of binder paper.

It was written in Taylor's straight, overly neat writing.

Dear everybody,

I have decided to run away. I'll be fine.

My brother Zack knows why.

I'll send for my robots and tools. Mail them carefully.

Thank you,

Taylor S. McGee, 1st grader

Principal Luntz peered down at me.

I stared at the note and tried not to look guilty.

"I do not like when my students run away from home, but when they run away from school, it causes me great difficulty. He indicates you know why he ran away. Can you shed some light on that?"

I twisted up my mouth and looked at the ceiling, trying to look like I was thinking of a reason Taylor might run away. "Not a clue," I concluded.

"Okay," he sighed, focusing on me with intense interest. "Have a seat. Your parents will be here in a minute or two."

That was grim news. As my mind raced, one thing remained clear: my brother could not take a joke.

51

08

The Drive

"You're not getting the gravity of this situation," Mom said, turning around in the front seat to check on how upset I looked.

I've found that there's nothing worse than getting the third degree in the car. There's no escape, no distractions, and you can't even hope to get sent to your room.

"Why's it my fault that Taylor is playing hooky?" I argued.

"Not hooky!" Mom exclaimed. "He ran away!"

"He left a note," Dad reminded me. "He blamed you."

"He didn't blame me," I corrected him. "He only said I knew why."

"So then: Why?" Dad growled for the fifth time.

"I told you," I said. "He's been listening in on me and Olivia. Spying on us. So we were just joking about spiders in the house. It was just a prank."

"Well, this is a fine mess you've got us into." My dad simmered as he white-knuckled the steering wheel.

"Taylor couldn't have gone far," I said. "His legs are too short, he doesn't have a wallet, and he can't even make his own sandwiches yet."

"He's my baby," Mom said. She was starting to cry now, which made me feel so much worse.

"He sure is acting like one," I mumbled under my breath.

"You'll have some answering to do later," Dad growled, staring me down in the rearview mirror.

"Can we at least turn on some music?" I asked. No response.

We were driving to Miles Tomlinson's house. He was Taylor's best friend. Mom kept calling their home number on her cell as she scanned the street. School wasn't out yet, so the streets and sidewalks of our neighborhood were deserted. Nobody picked up the phone at Miles's house.

"Even if he were there, I don't think he'd pick up their phone," I said. It was true, but they didn't seem to care.

The car got quiet, and I listened to the engine roar as Dad hit the gas pedal again.

"Principal Luntz is such a nice man," Mom finally commented, looking out the window as we zipped by homes and stores.

"Nice?" I yelped. "Principal Luntz is a total doozle," I said.

"Watch the language," Dad said.

"Language?" I cried. "That's not even English!"

"Yes, but I know what you meant by it."

I threw my hands up at that one and just sat

back and considered the possibility of running away myself.

It turned out that Taylor was not at Miles Tomlinson's house. Or Sutter Smith's. Or Jack Vollrath's. We also stopped by 7-Eleven, Donut Heaven, Big Eye Books, and the dog park. No sign of him.

"Can we at least pick up some burgers and fries?" I asked. "I'm starving."

"You are so insensitive," Mom snapped at me, her eyes red with worry.

"What?" I said. "I'm not insensitive; I'm starving."

"Can it," Dad said.

I rolled my eyes and listened to my stomach make noises like a newborn cat. We visited the bowling alley, Grogani's Electronics, the comic shop, and, for some inexplicable reason, the pet store.

No sign of the runaway squirt anywhere.

My parents seemed to get extra tense with every failed visit, so I kept my mouth shut.

Until I couldn't take it anymore.

"Maybe he's at home," I finally said. "He's probably already given up on his whole run-away-from-home-to-get-more-attention scheme."

My parents exchanged a look that told me they were shocked they had not thought of the same thing.

It was past our regular dinnertime when we pulled up in front of our house. Mom and Dad both jumped out and jogged into the house. I stayed in the car, slumped in the backseat. Somehow I knew he'd be here. Taylor just wasn't the runaway type.

They didn't come out to continue the search. That alone told me that Taylor was already home.

"I told you," I grumbled inside the empty car. "That pest should have to chip in for all the gas we just wasted."

09

No Promises

"**W**hat do you mean you're not done with my walkie-talkie?" I whisper-screamed before school on Friday morning. "The race is tomorrow morning, Amp! Principal Luntz wants us to report to the information booth by seven a.m."

"I'm breaking new ground here, Zack," he said, guarding the opening to my closet as best he could. "This isn't easy to do, you know. It's a tribute to Erdian know-how that I'm this close to making it work."

"But you promised me you'd be done by now, you big blue fibber," I said.

"I didn't 'promise,'" he said, making air quotes on the word *promise* with his mini, three-fingered hands. "I predicted I'd be done. Totally different."

"Oh my gosh, Amp, I can't show up without my

walkie-talkie! You can't get kicked off Young Volunteers! It's . . . it's like jail. You don't get thrown out of jail for bad behavior, they just make you stay longer—"

I caught a glimpse of my walkie-talkie. I gasped. Half the components on the little green board inside the walkie-talkie had been popped off. Wires stuck up at odd angles, attached to nothing. Other important-looking parts were scattered on the carpet. I stared in horror. "What the—? Did you blow it up, Amp?!"

"It's not as bad as it looks, Zack."

"*No?* It's probably worse than it looks."

"Don't worry," he said, waving a casual hand at the destruction behind him. "I know where everything goes. Pretty much."

I walked over to my bed and collapsed facedown onto it. I let out a groan. "I may be going to real prison when Principal Luntz gets his hands on me."

"I'm not sure you understand how difficult this is," he said from somewhere down on the carpet.

"Oh, I think I have a firm grasp of how difficult you are," I bellowed into the blanket pressed to my face.

"No, not me! I'm talking about the device I'm constructing."

I looked down at him. "Constructing? Seriously? I see a lot more demolition than construction in there, Dr. Frankenstein."

"Who?"

"Dr. Franken—oh, never mind! I forgot: Erdians have no sense of humor."

"I don't see what's funny about this situation."

"That's what I've been saying!" I glared at him. "What's more important? Stopping an alien invasion on Earth, or having a walkie-talkie so people can find the portable toilets?"

"Hey, that's pretty dang important when you've gotta go," I said. I sat up on the edge of the bed and considered my pint-size roommate. "Is there any way you can finish tonight and put everything back in its place by sunrise?"

"No."

I grunted. "Aren't you going to even think about it? At least pretend to think it's possible?"

He stared at me. Then tapped his foot, scratched his head, and made a weird humming sound for over a minute. "Okay, I thought about it."

"And?"

"No, I won't be done."

I fell back on my bed and rested an arm over my watery eyes. "This may be more stress than a fourth grader can handle."

10

Up and At 'Em

*C*LINK!
      PLINK!
CLICK!

I felt like someone was tapping on my dream.

I was dreaming that I was emptying my pockets as fast as I could, but they were stuffed with a never-ending supply of hairy tarantulas, walkie-talkie parts, and crumbling Ritz crackers.

I was sure this was something my mom would label an anxiety dream.

So I didn't mind someone knocking on my dream. I stopped my frantic emptying and looked at the growing pile of spiders, electronics, and crackers. Then I woke up.

TAP! CLICK!

My window. The noise was coming from my

window. I knew who was throwing pebbles against my window without having to look.

BANG!

Okay, now that one was a rock! What was she thinking?

I sat up. I stumbled to my window and yanked back the curtain. The sky was just starting to shake off the night, turning a soft violet color. I opened my window and leaned out.

The cold air hit me in the face like a cream pie.

"Whoa, you look like a dead rooster," Olivia called from down below. She had come through a hole in the backyard fence and now stood on the wet lawn, hands on hips and walkie-talkie clipped to her belt.

"I was having a bad dream," I mumbled. I started to shiver.

"I've been trying to call you on the walkie-talkie," she said, unclipping hers and waving it in the air.

"Why don't you answer?"

"Because Amp isn't done with it. It's still in a million pieces."

"*What?* Are you guys crazy?!" she scream-whispered. "Luntz will not be happy. He already doesn't like you, you know."

"I am aware of that," I said softly.

"You better tell him I had nothing to do with tearing that walkie-talkie apart."

"Don't worry," I whispered. "We'll cook up some kind of excuse."

"No, *you'll* cook up an excuse," she said, flapping her arms. "Don't involve me in your destruction of school property. You know, it's often not the crime itself that gets people in trouble, it's the cover-up that follows that does you in."

"Hold on," I snapped. "There's no crime here. No cover-up. Just take it down a notch, drama mama."

"Whatever," she said, folding her arms. "I'll visit you in prison. I promise."

I thought for a second. "I'll be down in two minutes." I closed my window and dressed in ten seconds.

I looked into the closet. The walkie-talkie

pieces were still scattered everywhere. Actually, it looked worse, which was truly startling considering how bad it looked last night. "Amp, you really messed me up on this one."

"I'm almost ready," a weary Amp called out from inside.

"Aaaagh," I grunted, and stomped off.

Outside my room, the hallway was stacked on both sides with stuff from Taylor's room. He was still doing a complete cleaning, despite the fact that I had been forced to admit to and apologize

for tricking him with Amp the spider. But my parents did take away his walkie-talkie receiver, so I considered the whole ordeal a partial victory.

I zipped down the stairs, jotted a quick note for my parents telling them I'd left early for the race, and headed out the door with visions of Principal Luntz's angry face dancing in my head.

11

Get Ready, Get Set, Panic!

By the time Olivia and I were riding our bikes around the corner at the end of our street, the sky was brightening from deep purple to light blue.

"Just tell him your dumb dog ate it," Olivia suggested.

"My dog . . . isn't dumb . . . and doesn't . . . eat . . . walkie-talkies," I huffed, my pumping legs already feeling like they were filled with small rocks. "My cat, maybe—"

Olivia gave me a look.

The air around us was still moist and cool, but you could feel the heat of the day working its fingers into the air.

Olivia shook her head. "Then tell him the tiny alien who secretly lives in your room needed your

walkie-talkie to radio his home planet and call off an epic invasion of Earth."

"The truth . . . is not . . . an option," I sputtered. "At least . . . wherever . . . Amp . . . is concerned." Gosh, I was in bad shape!

We were downtown in less than fifteen minutes. The preparations for the race were already well underway. A news van was setting up for a live report from the starting line. Police officers were setting up traffic barricades. EMTs were leaning on their vehicles, drinking coffee.

We parked behind the library. While I caught my breath, Olivia secured both of our bikes to the bike rack with an impressive-looking lock and chain.

We had arrived at the same time that two other kids from our class were dropped off, Nino Sasso and Max Myers. They approached us as Olivia finished locking up our bikes. I noted that Max had only one eye open.

"Half my brain is still asleep," Max mumbled. "And the other half is dreaming."

If anybody else had said this, it would have been funny, but Max was too big and scary to laugh around. Laughing at Max was dangerous.

We all walked to the information table to check in for the race. I noticed Nino and Max had their walkie-talkies. They didn't seem to notice my lack of one.

Olivia insisted she go first, with Nino and Max in line between us. She could be bossy that way.

My out-of-shape heart kicked into high gear again as I tried to decide how to break the news to Principal Luntz that my walkie-talkie—no, *his* walkie-talkie!—was torn apart and in about forty-five pieces. I watched as Luntz glanced at Olivia's walkie-talkie and made a mark on his clipboard. She turned from the table and walked right up to me.

"Good luck, McGee," she said, looking me in the eyes.

Without looking down, she pushed her walkie-talkie into my left hand. After a moment's hesitation, I took it. Oh! I was going to show Principal Luntz Olivia's walkie-talkie, like it was mine? Simple, yet so sneaky!

Sure enough, when it was my turn and Luntz said "Walkie-talkie?", I held up Olivia's. He barely glanced at it. He just made his check mark. "Good to see you up so early, McGee," he said.

It was all I could do not to do my happy dance.

I just peeled off from the front of the line and walked quickly back to a waiting Olivia. "He fell for it," I said.

"Of course he did," she said, taking her radio from me. She blew out a big breath. "You probably won't need a radio anyway. Portable toilets are over by the community center." She smiled at me. "Don't fall in," she said, and clapped me on the shoulder. She headed off for the racers' registration table, where she would be helping late-arriving runners turn in their paperwork and get their official runner's numbers.

Olivia was right: I didn't need a radio. I was instantly so busy guiding the growing crowd to the portable toilets, giving out directions to the hand-washing stations, and pointing lost runners toward the registration table that I forgot I had ever had a walkie-talkie.

Just as I thought this Young Volunteers assignment was going to go off without a hitch and Amp had won extra time to get his quantum radio in working order, I heard something that made my stomach dry up like a sponge.

"ZACK MCGEE, PLEASE REPORT TO THE REGISTRATION TABLE IMMEDIATELY!" the sound system blared. The voice was familiar but staticky. "ZACK MCGEE. REGISTRATION

TABLE. NOW!"

Me?

I stared up at the
speakers that were strung
above the closed-off street
where I stood. "Oh, no," was all
I could think to say.

As I made my way through the growing sea of
people, all of whom seemed to be rushing one
way or another—it really was a bit chaotic for
an early-morning race—I could only think that
Principal Luntz had somehow found out about my
destroyed radio.

I was so nervous I thought the truth might
finally become my only option.

12

Attention, Earth

"**W**hy didn't you answer your walkie-talkie?" Max Myers shouted at me.

The crowd was beginning to feel more like an unruly mob. People were moving in every direction imaginable. Max grabbed me before I reached the registration table. The crowd was now swarming with confusion, and it suddenly seemed very loud.

"Olivia told me to find you," Max yelled at me. He was holding me tightly by the shoulders. He seemed panicked. "She made me promise. I had to use the sound system. There's not a moment to spare!"

"Wait. Why?"

"She had to leave," he roared.

"But we just got here a half hour ago."

"I don't know. She just said something about

79

going to your friend's house," he said.

"Wait! What friend? What's going on, Max?"

"It must have something to do with the announcements!"

Just then, someone bumped me as they rushed past, but Max steadied me with his meaty hand.

"I don't get it," I said, leaning in to be heard. "What friend's house? What announcements?"

"She said you would know what friend," he said. "She was freaking out like everybody else. I don't know, this could be the end, McGee." Max pulled up his T-shirt collar and started chewing on it. He looked like he was in full panic mode.

As the crowd jostled and flowed around us, my mind raced. Amp? She went to see Amp? Why on earth would she leave a Young Volunteers event to see Amp? The world had suddenly gone totally bonkers.

"What did the announcements say, exactly?" I shouted.

"Someone or something keeps hacking into all the police radios, walkie-talkies, TV broadcasts—everything! That's why everybody's freaking out. I can't believe you didn't hear. Where's your radio?

I have a bad feeling about this stuff, McGee," Max said, pressing his beefy hands into the sides of his head. His eyes were watery. "If I don't see you again, it's been nice knowing you. I'm glad you were on my baseball team. You're a good team-mate. A good catcher." With that, Max gave me a bear hug that nearly snapped my spine.

"I'm so lost," I wheezed. "Are you moving or something, Max?"

He released me and stepped back. "That weird, squeaky voice that's been broadcasting says the alien attack will begin at any—"

"WHAT?! DID YOU SAY A SQUEAKY VOICE?" I hollered, grabbing Max by his boulder shoulders.

"Sorry, buddy," Max shouted, knocking my hands away with a two-armed flick. "I'm going home to be with my family. Might as well eat all the ice cream, since who knows if we'll make it through the—"

I was gone before he finished. Now I ran through the crowd, pushing my way when I had to. My brain felt like it was melting. I couldn't get enough air to my lungs.

I tried to think really hard, mentally telling Amp to shut up. Maybe he could hear my thoughts, but as soon as I started I knew it was a dumb idea. He might be able to do that in my room, but not in this crazy crowd all the way downtown.

I just needed my bike. I hoped Olivia had thought to leave my bike unlocked. I finally broke free from the buzzing swarm of humanity as I rounded the corner of the library. I sprinted to the bike rack. I'd ride as fast as I could and be home in ten minutes.

But both our bikes were still locked up! *What?!*

Just then the crowd seemed to stop. They all froze and looked up. The air filled with Amp's high-pitched voice. It seemed to come from every direction at once. It filled the air like squeaky thunder.

"ATTENTION, ERDIAN COUNCIL! CALL OFF THE INVASION OF EARTH BY THE ERDIAN FORWARD GUARD. THIS IS ADVANCED SCOUT AMP OF THE SPACE CRUISER *DINGLE*. I REPEAT, CALL OFF

83

THE INVASION OF EARTH. RECALL THE FIRST-WAVE INVASION STRIKE FORCE IMMEDIATELY! PLEASE CONFIRM RECEIPT. OVER."

The world around me was plunged into silence. Nobody moved.

I stared, open-mouthed into the air like I was in a trance.

"What did you do to my walkie-talkie?" I whispered.

As soon as I said it, I heard the crowd gasp. Someone even shrieked. I realized I had never heard a real-life shriek before.

"Hey, kid!" someone shouted from behind me.

I whipped around, thinking Principal Luntz was about to grab me by the back of my T-shirt.

It was a police officer. I instantly imagined he had been looking for me and would now handcuff me for all the trouble Amp and I were causing.

Amp's broadcast must have stopped him in his tracks like everyone else on the street. He looked from me to the radio and back to me. "Kid, you better get yourself home. I don't know what's going on, but we may be attacked by aliens at any moment."

I couldn't speak. Technically, he was right, but I couldn't dip my toe into the truth now. So without another word, I turned and ran off.

"Is this really happening?" I gasped, as I became just another panicky citizen running around like a headless chicken.

Strangely, the only other thought that bounced around in my head as I chugged up the slope of Main Street was that Amp was clearly the worst roommate in history.

13

The Road Home

I was in terrible condition.

My lungs felt like they were the size of grapes. Squished grapes. That had dried out in the sun for a week. So I guess they felt like raisins.

What seemed like just minutes when Olivia and I were on our bikes now seemed like three half marathons strung together.

It seemed like the entire town was outside, looking up. I saw all manner of people out on their lawns watching the skies. They had telescopes, binoculars, fancy cameras with long lenses, and smartphones with built-in video cameras. Some families were quickly packing up their cars, like they were leaving town in a hurry to escape the incoming Erdian space invaders.

This was nuts!

As I huffed and chuffed down the middle of the street, people called out the strangest warnings to me.

"Go the other way. You're headed right into their trap, boy!" a man hollered at me.

"Stop running so fast!" a woman yelled. "Aliens are attracted to movement."

"Kid, put some goggles on to hide your eyes. Aliens always eat the eyes first! They taste like chicken!"

Huh?

I also overheard two nervous women speaking quietly as I ran by. "Sure, he looks like a regular kid, but he could be one of them in disguise, one of those body-snatching aliens."

To which the other woman replied, "If he tries to eat our eyes, I will sock him in the face. No alien is gonna mess with my street."

What? This was getting downright dangerous!

Amp was right: humans were unpredictable.

Police cars, fire trucks, ambulances, news vans, and then the city dogcatcher zipped past me at unsafe speeds. Weirdly, these were soon followed by an ice-cream truck, which thundered by at about eighty miles an hour. That couldn't be good for business. As it rumbled past, I heard its jingling tune get interrupted by Amp's urgent voice. This time it wasn't in English, it was in Erdian, which sounded like a frog being stepped on repeatedly. Because I knew him, I could tell that Amp sounded desperate. Or frustrated. No, he sounded really annoyed. I even heard him say "floofy" at some point. I'm sure he was starting to realize that his lame walkie-talkie plan was failing miserably. The question was, would he shut up before anyone got hurt or run over to death by a nervous ice-cream truck driver?

I was slick with sweat and incredibly thirsty when I finally rounded the corner of my street. The growing heat of the day was cooking me slowly, like a tiny boy in a giant crockpot.

And then I stopped dead in my tracks.

It was crawling with cops and news vans!

They were everywhere!

I saw several men wearing headphones attached to those inside-out umbrella thingies. They were walking around, scanning the street, and I knew just what they were doing: they were closing in on the signal of whoever was broadcasting the ridiculous alien invasion news that was panicking the entire town.

They were closing in on Amp and my dang walkie-talkie!

And when they found Amp . . . then you'd really see adults in a panic. They would think the invasion was already underway (which, I suppose, technically, it actually kinda was).

I shot up the nearest driveway and decided I'd secretly make my way up the street to my own backyard by way of my neighbors' yards. Nobody would see me coming.

The bad news was my legs were rubbery with exhaustion, and the idea of hopping fences right now seemed impossible.

The good news was that I was in such a panic, I wasn't feeling any pain, only desperation.

14

Get Up for It

You wouldn't think getting to your house by running through six backyards would be all that difficult. I've done it a thousand times before. But today, it wasn't just difficult, it was downright life-threatening.

The first few backyards weren't bad. I was chased by a nasty poodle named Luna, I stomped through a strawberry garden, and I almost broke my foot on a cement tortoise lawn decoration thingy, but it wasn't anything I couldn't handle.

But in the Swopes' backyard, things got loopy. I was flying through some laundry that had been hung out to dry—who still did that?—and didn't see the hot tub on the other side of the drying laundry.

I've never felt strongly that hot tubs should be

covered when not in use, but falling into practically boiling water with a pillowcase wrapped around your head changes your view of things.

"AAAGH!" I screamed when I emerged like the Swamp Thing from the soup-hot water. I threw off the pillowcase and fell to the ground. I grabbed my throbbing right thigh, which had smashed into the seat ledge just under the water's surface. I had received the worst charley horse in the history of legs and charley horses.

Sopping wet and steaming hot, I pushed forward like a half-cooked water buffalo, crawling over a patch of dirt to the fence. Of course, the dirt stuck to me. And in seconds I realized that the dirt was from a recently planted garden that must have been sprinkled with fertilizer, what a farmer might call manure—or what you and I would call poop.

I arrived in my backyard wild-eyed, huffing and puffing, limping, sopping wet, and smelling like a four-foot-tall cow patty.

Once my feet were firmly planted in my own backyard, I was instantly tackled from behind.

"Get down!" Olivia grunted in my ear. "They're everywhere."

"You almost broke my back," I wheezed through gritted teeth.

"Why are you so wet? Is that sweat?!"

"No, it's hot tub."

"Oh my gosh, you smell like poop! Did you have an accident?"

I rolled onto my knees and caught my breath. "That's not important," I growled.

"Says you!" she hissed, covering her mouth and nose. "Your stink is makin' me blink."

"Forget that! We need to shut Amp up," I growled.

"I've been calling up to your bedroom window, but that pipsqueak can't hear me."

"Because he's set up in my closet," I said, getting into a limp crouch. "Let's go through the back door."

"No, the cops are downstairs. Your dad is talking to them now."

"*What?!* They'll find Amp!"

"I know," Olivia said, throwing her arms in the air. She looked up at the window and shook her head. She shrugged again. "Now what?"

"Let's get your grandpa's big ladder!" I said.

Keeping low, I slipped through the hole in the fence that stood between our two houses.

"Nice thinking," Olivia whispered from behind me.

We grabbed the ladder from the garage, tossed it over the fence, slid back through, and, like a trained team of firefighters, we had the ladder up to my window within thirty seconds flat. I started up first, but Olivia pushed past.

"Outta the way," she said, scrambling past me like a circus chimp.

She dove in through my open window, which was still missing its screen from the day Amp first crash-landed into my life. I heard her fall onto my desk and send my stuff crashing to the floor.

"Hey, take it easy in there," I hissed up the ladder. "There's homework on my desk that I really don't want to have to redo."

Seconds later her fist appeared at the top of the ladder. "Here, catch," she called out and released her fingers. A screaming Amp fell at me like a tiny blue bomb. I caught him as gently as I could and stuffed him in my pocket.

"Nice," Olivia said from somewhere in my

room. "You should
play baseball."

I growled but
didn't have the
energy to argue.

"Why is it
so wet in here?"
Amp croaked from
my pocket.

Before I could answer,
my walkie-talkie came flying out the window and
soared over my head. I watched it crash-land in
the grass. By the time I looked up again, Olivia
was coming back down the ladder almost as fast
as Amp had fallen.

I heard my dad's voice through my open window calling up the stairs for my brother. "Taylor,
are you making some kind of broadcast? Get down
here right now, please. The police are here!"

I didn't wait to hear Taylor's answer. Like the
Hunchback of Notre Dame, I limped across the
backyard and through the fence.

"You do know you smell like dead animals,
right?" Amp asked from my pocket.

I didn't answer. My head was spinning, my thigh was throbbing, and the cops were everywhere.

The relief finally washed over me as we opened the side door of Olivia's garage and closed it behind us with a quiet click.

Olivia and I exchanged a look and shook our heads. This was insane, but we were safe. Amp was safe. And we had the radio—well, at least what was left of it.

My only regret? I wished I could have seen Taylor's face when the cops accused him of causing a major citywide panic.

15

Post-disaster Review

"**P**erhaps I made the signal too strong," Amp said, puzzled.

"You think?" Olivia said, rolling her eyes.

"Amp, your voice was everywhere," I said.

We were sitting on the old couch in Olivia's garage. Amp stood in front of us on a cardboard box labeled GIVEAWAY CLOTHES. With the garage door closed and the light off, it was calm and peaceful in there after the insanity of just a few minutes earlier. But it smelled really bad, which was apparently my fault.

"Something went wrong," he said, staring up at the fishing poles.

"Oh, you have an amazing grasp of the obvious," I said. "And I heard you speaking Erdian, which is kinda gross-sounding. No offense."

101

He looked at me, but didn't say anything.

"It was a rather surprising turn of events," he said after a pause, pressing his three-fingered hands on the top of his head. "I'm not sure what went wrong."

"Epic fail, Short Pants," Olivia said, tapping the cardboard box with her foot.

"Don't call me that," Amp said, like a second grader. "I don't wear pants."

"Yeah, what's up with that, No Pants?" I said, and laughed quietly.

Amp suddenly looked like he remembered something. He turned his back to us and moved his wrist recorder to his face.

"Note to Erdian Council: Perhaps the broad-spectrum frequency repeater from the Dingle was too powerful. My experiment seems to have interrupted and overridden almost every frequency in use here. But the strength seems to have been focused terrestrially, on the surface, and not through a

**quantum connection.
Total mission fail."**

"Is there any way we can get you to stop doing that?" I asked.

"Sadly, no," he sighed, distracted.

Olivia nudged his box again with her foot. "Hey, we're all friends here, why do you have to turn your back to us? It's kinda creepy."

Amp blinked at us. "I don't know. Your faces are distracting."

"Distracting?" Olivia said, pretending to be offended. "Thanks for the compliment. Yours isn't exactly comforting either."

"Listen," Amp said, "the important thing is our secret is safe. As Zack would say, no harm, no foul."

I sat up. "You forgot about the part where you destroyed my walkie-talkie. And I got a charley horse so bad my grandchildren will feel it. That's a big foul."

"I could've put that walkie-talkie back together again, if Olivia hadn't flung it from your second-story window."

Olivia shook her head at him. "Maybe I should have flung *you*. And maybe you'd like to explain to Principal Luntz what happened."

Amp rubbed his tiny hands together. "That will be my pleasure. I can make him think he broke it."

"No," I said. "No more messing with minds. As soon as the street clears, we have to go back to the race. I'll think of something. Amp is right. The important thing is he didn't get discovered and dragged away."

Olivia shrugged. "Yeah, but as far as we know the invasion is still on."

I blew out a big breath and ran my fingers through my still-damp hair. "Let's just deal with Luntz and the walkie-talkie today. Tomorrow we'll deal with the Erdian invasion of Earth."

"At least you have your priorities in order," Olivia said, and made a face.

"Now, Amp," I said, "get off of that box. I need to borrow some clothes that won't make me gag."

16

No Jury, No Trial

"**S**o you didn't leave Olivia's ladder on the side of the house?" my dad asked, watching my face like a hawk.

As you might imagine, dinner at my house that night was tense. Everyone was squinting at me with suspicion. I tried my best to stay cool and casual.

I pretended to think about it for a second. "I don't remember using a ladder."

"But wouldn't you remember if you did?" Mom asked pointedly.

"I would think so," I said, trying my best not to be specific. I could feel my parents' eyeballs watching me as I pushed string beans around my plate with my fork.

"Well, I know it wasn't me the cops were after," Taylor said, quietly. "And the ladder didn't

go up to my window. It went up to yours."

I looked at each one of them. "Hey, I was at the race. You can ask Max Myers. I don't know what else to say to you guys."

"And why are you dressed like that again?" Dad asked. "You look like a rodeo clown."

I looked down. I was wearing a giant pair of shorts with about thirty pockets and a huge shirt with GONE FISHING written across the chest. I had pulled the clothes out of the cardboard box in Olivia's garage. They were way too big, but they didn't smell half as bad as mine, which were now in the garbage can in Olivia's garage.

"Oh, I borrowed these," I said, skimming off the truth for the first time. "My other clothes got stuff all over them. The situation was pretty hectic. Some guy hacked into all the radios and stuff. Wacky."

"And Mr. Luntz says that's how your walkie-talkie got broken," Mom said.

"Oh, yeah," I said, not realizing my mom had talked to Luntz. "It got knocked out of my hands and trampled on. It was crazy. You guys have no idea."

My parents looked at each other. I wasn't sure if my story was holding together. I took no pleasure in fibbing like this, but I figured it was the only way I could keep Amp a secret.

"I told Mr. Luntz you'd do another year in Young Volunteers," Mom announced.

"You did what?!"

"Ha, ha . . . ," Taylor sang.

"It only seemed fair," Dad said firmly, putting down his fork and fixing me with his dinner look. "Especially with what you've put your brother through with this spider business. Consider it a punishment if you want."

"Bummer," Taylor said gleefully.

I was too shocked to speak.

"Your father had to spray for bugs three times," Mom said, looking at Taylor with a sad smile. "Poor baby."

I gripped the edge of the table. "Him? *Him* poor baby? What about me? You just sent me to prison for another year! I was so close to escaping from that lousy club."

"It only seemed fair, dear," Mom cooed. "Principal Luntz seemed quite flustered about his walkie-talkie getting destroyed. He actually said all the parts were ripped out of it, like someone was mad at it or something."

"That's odd," Dad said, staring at me.

I shrugged. I wasn't going to say anything else. I really was a terrible liar. And the web I was weaving was getting a little too complex to keep track of. Plus, we had avoided disaster and that's what counted. I'd just have to do my time in the Young Volunteers with quiet determination.

At least Amp was safe, and we still had time to call off the invasion. I had to keep my eye on the prize. Focus on the big picture. Saving all of humanity from an extraterrestrial invasion was more important than working for Luntz for another twelve months. It was close, but . . .

I shuddered at the thought of it.

I jerked a bit when I heard Amp's voice inside my head. It was one of his favorite Erdian Jedi mind tricks, but I never got used to it. "Thank you, Zack. I'm sorry I made a mess of things. I'll make it up to you."

"That's what has me worried," I said aloud.

My family all looked up at me in surprise. I

hadn't meant to say it out loud. I smiled crookedly and went back to my string beans, which I hated. I shoveled in a heaping forkful and gave my family a big, fake smile. When you stash a secret alien your room, you've got to learn to take a few for the team.

At that moment I knew being in the Young Volunteers for another year was going to be the least of my problems.

I needed to get my roommate off this planet if it was the last thing I did.

And there was a good chance that it just might be.

The End

Try It Yourself: Building Your Own Radio

In *Radio Active*, Amp realizes that the clock-gadget he's got on his wrist provides him with a powerful link back to Erde: his clock gives the exact time on his home planet because it works by quantum entanglement, which Einstein described as "spooky action at a distance." It's hard to perform quantum entanglement at home, but we can easily make a one-way radio link that works almost as well. To broadcast your own voice recording or music to a nearby AM radio, only a few components are needed. The first is an audio transformer that will help strengthen the signal you're going to broadcast. The second is an oscillator, which provides the modulation of the signal, and the broadcasting. Of course you'll need some wire to hook things up, and a 1/8" audio jack to plug into your music player or phone. Last, you'll need a 9 V battery and snap, so you can hook up the power.

AM Radio Transmitter Parts List

8 ohm to 1000 ohm Audio Transformer (Radio Shack 273–1380 or equivalent)

1 MHz Oscillator (Digi-Key X101-ND or equivalent)

1/8" audio plug with wires attached (Digi-Key CP-2205-ND or equivalent)

9 V battery snap with wires attached (Digi-Key BS61-ND or equivalent)

Single-conductor hookup wire, 22 to 28 gauge

A Note Before Getting Started

Get an adult to help you. You may need to use a soldering iron. It's the best way to connect wires in electronics projects. (You can also carefully twist the wires together, but make sure to twist the wires tightly! Make them into an even "Y" shape, then twist the arms of the Y.) You may also need to strip the insulation off your wires. You'll need a wire stripping tool to do this.

No matter how careful you are, accidents can happen. This is why it's essential that you have an adult's help.

1. Hook up the audio plug to the 8 ohm side of the transformer

    Most transformers will have a little diagram on the back that says which wires are which. You'll want to connect the audio plug to the 8 ohm side of the transformer, which is the side that has only 2 wires coming off of it. Twist one wire together with the first wire coming out of the plug's cable, and the second wire to the second plug cable. There may be a ground connection coming out of the plug cable, too—it will look different from the other two. You don't have to connect it to anything.

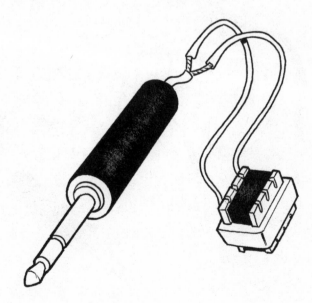

117

2. Hook up the transformer to the 9 V battery + wire (colored red)

The 9 V battery snap will have two wires coming off—one red and one black. Twist the red wire to one of the end wires on the 1000 ohm side of the transformer. There are three wires coming off on the 1000 ohm side, which is the opposite side from the 8 ohm one where you just wired in the audio plug.

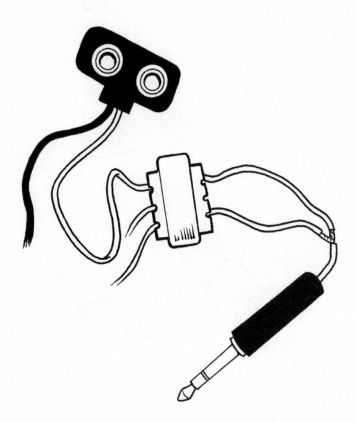

3. Hook up the transformer to the 1 Mhz Oscillator

Take the other end wire on the 1000 ohm side of the transformer and twist it to the top-left pin of the oscillator. You can tell when it's the top-left one because when you're looking at the top of the oscillator with its pins going downward, the bottom-left corner (pin 1) is the corner that's extra square looking. You want the pin above that one. Check out the diagram if you're not sure.

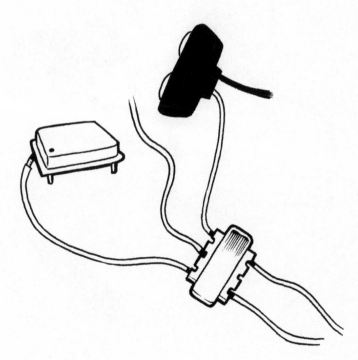

4. Attach the 9 V battery wire (colored black) to the 1 Mhz Oscillator

Take the black wire coming from your 9 V battery, and twist it onto the bottom-right pin on the oscillator. Remember to keep the extra-square corner as the bottom-left pin when looking down at the top.

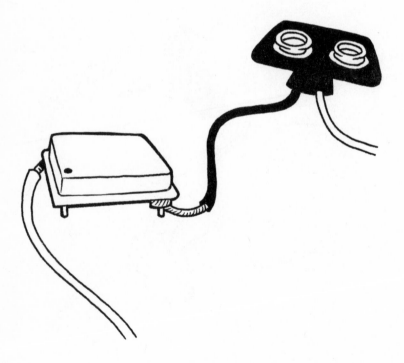

5. Hook up the Antenna to the 1 Mhz Oscillator

Last step: cut off a few inches of wire and twist them onto the top-right pin of the oscillator. As a reminder, the middle wire on the transformer and the bottom-left pin of the oscillator are not used in this circuit, so don't worry that they're not connected to anything. Now you're ready to try it!

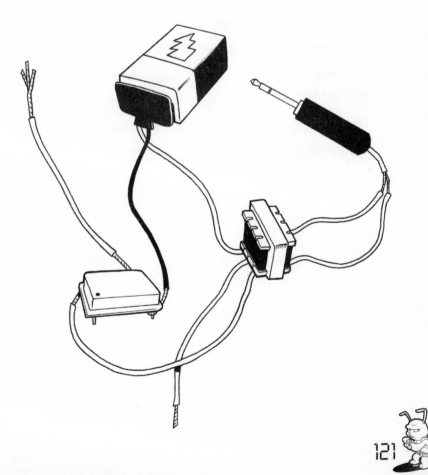

Using the Transmitter

1. To pick up the signal you're transmitting, you need an AM radio. Tune the AM radio to 1000. This is the transmission frequency, driven by your 1 MHz Oscillator. Insert the 1/8" plug into your phone or MP3 player and turn up the volume all the way. You may need to turn up the volume on the AM radio pretty high, too.

   Turn on a song on your phone or music player, and you should be able to hear it coming through the AM radio! This is a very low-power design, so you might need to start with them only a few inches apart to get it going.

Troubleshooting

Like any project, it might not work perfectly on the first try. Troubleshooting (sometimes called "debugging" for an electronics project like this) is a skill in itself that's important to learn. Amp needs to do it himself, in fact, to get his quantum link working! Here are some things to try if you're not hearing the transmission when you power everything up:

* **Make sure all your connections are good**
  When twisting wires together for electrical connections, things might not always be conducting electricity the way you want. Make sure all your connections are twisted very tightly.

* **Tune the radio carefully**
  If the radio isn't right on 1000 Khz exactly, you probably won't hear the signal coming through. Try turning the dial slowly back and forth near 1000 Khz.

* **Turn up the volume**
  The transmitter will work best when the MP3

player or phone is at max power, so turn the volume all the way up. Also try turning up the volume on the radio itself.

- **Check the connections**
  If it's not hooked up right, it definitely won't work. Compare your circuit to the one shown in the diagram. Do they match exactly? If not, see what you need to fix.

Once your transmitter is working, try recording your own message to call off an alien attack with the voice recorder on your phone, and transmit it to the AM radio! If you're lucky, the Erdians will hear you and go back home. Good luck!

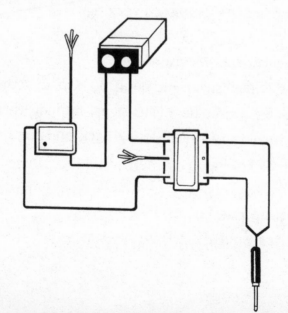

Read a sneak peek of book four
of the Alien in My Pocket series:

On Impact!

My legs are spaghetti.

Or socks filled with pancake batter.

Or octopus tentacles.

Or wait: soggy wet beach towels.

That's it: my legs are soggy octopus tentacles in dress socks filled with spaghetti and pancake batter.

At least that's what it felt like as I rode my bike to school. I was exhausted.

And Amp was to blame for it all, of course.

He made me miss my bus . . . again! Third time in one week. That was a new record.

My dad drove me to school the first two times, but this time he had a big presentation at work.

So there I was, riding my bike as fast as I could to get to a spelling test that I hadn't studied for.

My life was a mess. Before my pesky blue alien crash-landed his crummy spaceship into my bedroom, I had a fairly regular life. I played baseball.

1

I got decent grades. I slept eight to ten hours a night. Now I had Amp to worry about. It's like he travelled a bajillion miles through space and time just to get on my nerves. And oh, yeah, to scout Earth to see if it was worth invading.

My best friend, Olivia, is the only other person who knows about Amp, but she gets to go home at the end of the day.

Here's some friendly advice: never adopt an alien. Trust me.

I leaned into the corner of Jacob Drive at full speed and my overly stuffed backpack almost sent me spilling to the pavement.

That's when I saw them up ahead in the middle of the street: a pack of hulking black crows standing around like a gang of misfits waiting to steal my lunch money.

Crows gave me the creeps. I don't know why, but they made me uneasy. They were bad news . . . with wings.

I leaned over my handlebars, tapped into whatever strength remained in my watery legs, and rode right at them. They squawked and screeched and flew out of my way at the last possible second. "HA!" I shouted. "Out of the street, you turkeys!"

Seconds later, I roared up to the bike racks outside of Reed Elementary School. I felt like a knight returning from a successful battle, ready to give the king good news.

But my smile disappeared almost instantly.

My bike wasn't slowing down. I squeezed the brake levers on my handlebars. Nothing. I had no brakes! I was going full speed at the first bike rack!

One last thought shot through my brain before impact: THIS IS YOUR FAULT, AMP!

At least I had gotten out of the spelling test.

I was now lying in my bed trying like crazy to find a silver lining.

I wasn't dead.

And the arm that now hung in a sling wasn't my throwing arm. If you're going to dislocate your shoulder, it's best not to destroy your baseball career at the same time.

The phone rang. I could hear my mom say hello to Coach Lopez. "Apparently, somebody stole his bike brakes," she explained to him. "I know—weird. But Zack wanted me to mention that it's his left arm. His throwing arm sustained no damage. He even wrote that down for me. How cute is that?"

"Mom!" I yelled down, and she stopped her conversation and said, "Yes, Zacky?" But I couldn't think of how to tell her that she wasn't supposed to tell him that she was reading my instructions without making matters worse! "Nothing." I sighed, and she went back to talking to Coach Lopez while I propped myself up in my bed.

My head was loopy from the pain pills. I felt mentally jumbled. My brain kept wandering off.

My skull felt like it was filled with lemonade and goldfish.

But at least my shoulder didn't hurt too badly.

I wondered if my little bike rack incident would make the yearbook. That'd be so embarrassing, but also kind of cool if they gave my accident a whole page.

Luckily, classes were about to start when the ambulance finally arrived, but a decent-sized crowd had still hung around. I remember hearing the mix of different voices as I lay wedged between two bikes.

"Is he dead?" someone wondered.

"Who taught that idiot how to ride a bike?"

"Don't be mean—maybe he's blind."

"That's ridiculous, why would a blind kid ride a bike to school?"

"Who is it?"

"I think it's Shane Kerr."

"No, that's Debbie Finster," another kid corrected her. He sounded so sure. "Her dad is my dentist."

"Oh, yeah, that was Debbie for sure," a girl said sadly. I took particular interest in her use of the past tense.

5

Principal Luntz was the first adult on the scene. "I should have known it would be you, Zack McGee," was all he said. He shook his head at me with a frown, as if I had meant to pop my arm bone from its socket just to avoid a spelling quiz.

The ride in the back of an ambulance was pretty what you'd expect: it smelled like medicine, you couldn't see where you were going, and they didn't play music. Apparently, a dislocated shoulder doesn't merit using the siren, which was a little disappointing.

Now here I was, in my bed, my baseball season ruined—and I had a combination lemonade stand and aquarium open for business in my head.

I hadn't seen the hamster-sized alien who'd made me late in the first place since I got home. He was probably hiding. Amp knew he'd get an earful when he came out. I didn't remember dozing off, but I must have.

I dreamed of crows chewing the brakes off my bike as I served them cups of cold lemonade poured directly from my nose.

Maybe we should start breaking those big white pain pills in half.

The most annoying thing about living with an alien is the impact it has on your sleep.

Since Amp's crippled spaceship dented my bedroom wall, getting a good night's sleep had become about as likely as catching a one-eyed unicorn that burps rainbows and farts lightning.

On the planet Erde, there's no such thing as sleep. Amp doesn't understand why I need it. He ignores my complaints about being woken up all the time. It's like living with a misfiring cuckoo clock.

But thanks to the mind-bending pain pills, I actually had a full night's rest. Even a four-inch-tall alien on my chest couldn't wake me before I was ready.

"It's about time," Amp said in his strange, high-pitched voice.

"Thanks for your concern about my arm," I said with a sigh.

"Yes, I see you have a boo-boo."

"A boo-boo? I almost died!"

"That device on your arm doesn't indicate a severe injury," he said, stroking his chin.

"Oh, thanks a lot, Doctor Amp," I said. "I have

a rash I'd like you to take a look at when you're done."

"Whoa! Grumpy . . ."

"You're to blame for all this, you know."

"Me? What did I do?"

"You made me late for school."

"How exactly did I do that?"

"Let's start with the fact that your people are about to invade Earth. That doesn't help." I ran my fingers through my hair with the hand from my good arm. "Plus, somebody stole the brake cables on my bike. That's why I crashed."

I waited for sympathy, but Amp was silent. "What's wrong?" I asked. "You look gassy. Please don't fart right now. I'm not sure I can run away."

"You rode your bike?" he said in a faraway voice. "You never ride your bike on school days."

"I know, but I missed the bus. Remember? I was helping you fix a switch on your lame rocket-ship."

"But I thought your father was going to drive you!"

"He already drove me twice this week. He said my lateness was a character flaw."

"You can't argue with that," Amp said quietly.

"Whatever. He had a big presentation and couldn't drive me, and Mom had already left for work."

Amp was now pacing in front of the alarm clock. I could see it was 11:30 am. Wow, that really was a good night's sleep!

"I should have told you."

"Told me what?"

"I borrowed those brake wires when you were at school on Monday."

"Why on Earth would you do that!?!" I shouted.

"As you know, my landing system didn't function when I arrived here, so I was trying to fix the breaking flaps on my . . ." His voice trailed off when he saw the look on my face. He backed farther away from me. "Easy now, Zack." He looked nervous. "Remember, you have a boo-boo."

"I should have known it was you," I said between gritted teeth.

With a groan, I started to get up, but pain shot through my shoulder. He instantly disappeared from sight, using one of his alien mind-control abilities.

9

"Your Jedi tricks don't work on me anymore, Amp," I said. It was true; I had been teaching myself how to to deflect his invisible brain signals. At that instant, I saw him scamper across my bookshelf. "I SEE YOU!"

He sort of blinked on and off in my vision as I concentrated on blocking his mind trick. He dove off the bookshelf and ran across the carpet and into the closet.

"You better hide, you little blue headache."

Honestly, my arm hurt too much to actually chase him. It hurt just to swing my legs off my bed. I stared at the wall, my anger at Amp boiling.

Just then, there was a knock on my door

"Zack, it's time for your pill, and you have a visitor," Mom sang through the door.

I knew who the visitor was before the door opened.

"Come on in, Olivia," I groaned.